MW01124463

Amish

Homecoming

The Promise

Samantha Bayarr

Amish Homecoming: The Promise

Copyright © Samantha Bayarr 2019

Scripture quotations are from the New King James Version of the Bible.

Two broken promises equal one
broken heart for Sadie.

Seth has left the community and Sadie's father does
everything in his power to keep him away from his
daughter, including forcing her to marry Jed, a man
who is not kind to her.

Will she and Seth find their way back to each other, or
will Jesse, Jed's sister, get her hooks in him first?

GLOSSARY

ach: oh

aenti: aunt

boppli: baby

brudder: brother

danki: thank you

dat: father, dad

dawdi: grandfather

dochder: daughter

Englisher: a person who is not Amish

Fraa: wife

Frau: married woman

Freinden: friends

Gude mariye: good morning

gut: good

haus: house

jah: yes

kaffi: coffee

kapp: prayer cap

kinner: children

kume: come

mei: my

mamm: mom, mother

narrish: crazy, foolish

naerfich: nervous

onkel: uncle

Ordnung: rules of the Amish faith

Schweschder: sister

Wilkum: welcome

A NOTE FROM THE AUTHOR

While this story is set against the real backdrop of an Amish community in Indiana, the characters and the town are fictional. There is no intended resemblance between the characters and community in this story and any real members of the Amish or communities in Indiana. As with any work of fiction, I've taken license in some areas of research as a means of creating the necessary circumstances for my characters and the community in which they live. My research and experience with the Amish of Indiana are quite knowledgeable; however, it would be impossible to be entirely accurate in details and description since every community differs, and I have not lived near enough the Amish community for several years to know pertinent and current details. Therefore, any inaccuracies in the Amish lifestyle and their community portrayed in this book are due to fictional license as the author.

Thank you for being such a loyal reader.

TABLE OF CONTENTS

CHAPTER ONE

Sadie Beiler curled up in the loft of the barn and cried quietly. It wasn't fair that her father was trying to force her to marry Jedediah Bontrager just because he asked her; she didn't love him. Truthfully, she didn't even like him. He was immature and conceited; there was no denying he was good-looking, beautiful even. Anyone with a pair of eyes could see his outer qualities, but his insides were lacking.

"You need to stop waiting around for Seth and face the fact he isn't coming back," her father had said. *"Even if he did, I would forbid you to marry him because the way his vadder left the community and broke away from the church."*

Her father's words had cut right through her; Seth had promised he'd come back for her and they would be married, but she'd not heard a word from him in more than a year.

Maybe Dat is right, and I need to put away Seth, but I won't marry Jed.

Sadie sobbed even harder; she didn't care that Jed was likely on his way over to pick her up for a date.

Let him see me in here crying over Seth; maybe he'll go away and leave me alone.

Tabby nudged her and then curled up next to her and began to purr. She reached up and scratched the cat's head. *"Ach,* you understand how I feel, don't you, Tabby?"

Sadie wrapped her arms around the cat and cried into her fur. "What am I going to do if *Dat* forces me to marry Jed?"

"You'll learn to live with it, and you'll like it!" Jed's voice startled her.

Lifting her head, she peered down from the loft at Jed; how had he come in the barn without her hearing him?

"Go away, Jed and leave me alone," she cried. "I didn't invite you here."

"*Nee,* your *vadder* did," he said, annoyance in his tone. "So why don't you come down here at once and dry your eyes so we can be on our way? I won't have you embarrassing me out in public with your weepy, pity-party!"

"I don't have to do what you say," she said, sniffling.

Jed pursed his lips and blew out a loud sigh. "You better get used to obeying me, or you will not have an easy time being married to me."

"What is that supposed to mean?"

"It means that I won't have *mei fraa* pining over another *mann!*" he said through gritted teeth.

Sadie buried her face in the cat and bawled louder.

"*Dochder!*"

Sadie's head flew up when she heard her father's stern voice.

"Come down from there right now and do what you're supposed to do," he scolded her.

"*Dat,* please don't make me…"

"As long as you live under this roof you will do as I say!"

She wiped her eyes on her apron and slowly made her way down the ladder to the floor below; she curled her shoulders forward and hugged her middle, her eyes cast down. Her breath came out in short bursts, her shaky legs wanting her to bolt from the barn, but her father would punish her severely if she did.

Sadie walked slowly behind Jed, who was smirking like a spoiled child who'd gotten his way. How could she get out of marrying this smug man when she didn't have any way to live on her own? Her cousin had run off to

12

avoid an arranged marriage, and she'd lived in the streets for two weeks because she ran out of money; she finally came home and married the man her parents wanted her to marry, and she hasn't been the same since. Sadie didn't want to end up like her cousin, who had no hope in her eyes anymore.

Lord, please help me to find a way out of marrying Jedediah; I don't love him, and I worry it would be a sin to marry a man I didn't love. Keep me from sinning in this way and protect me from this arranged marriage. You know my heart is with Seth—the love of my youth. Please provide a way for me to wait for him; if he is on his way, put swiftness under his feet so he might get to me in time. Danki, Amen.

She followed Jed to his buggy and looked back at her father, who was standing by with his hands folded over his chest, waiting for her to obey him. It put resentment in her; she wished her mother would stand behind her, but she'd always let her husband make her decisions for her. Sadie didn't intend to be a rebellious wife, but she didn't believe a mother should choose sides against her child. Seth would never demand such a thing from her; he was a fair man. At least he was a few years ago when he'd promised to come back for her. Had he found someone else to love and would never come back for her?

She prayed not.

Jed hopped into the buggy and waited for Sadie to climb in; he wasn't even going to assister the way a gentleman should? She sighed, thinking it was better that way; if he touched her hand, she feared she might gag.

Once she was settled in the bench seat of his open buggy, she scooted over as far from Jed as possible.

"You don't have to be shy with me," he said with a chuckle. "You're my betrothed now so we can cuddle."

She flashed him a challenging look; she would jump out of his buggy if he put his hands on her in the least. She only intended to go along with this forced match until God answered her prayers.

Sadie kept quiet the entire ride into town, not wanting to encourage Jed in any way.

"Where would you like to go for our date?" he asked.

She shrugged, but then she spotted a *Help Wanted* sign in the window of the bakery and had a sudden urge to stop there. Would a job help her to get out of this? If she worked and paid her own way instead of living under her father's roof, she wouldn't have to live by his rules.

"My stomach is a little sore, but I think maybe we could go to the bakery and get some tea and a scone," she suggested. "Then we could walk around the park; it's such a lovely day."

He patted her leg, and she flinched away from him. "I think that's a *gut* idea; I'm happy to see you aren't trying to make this date miserable for me. I'd hate to have to tell your *vadder* you aren't obeying me."

Sadie resisted every urge in her to retort his comment; after all, if she was going to get into that bakery to inquire about the job, she needed to lure him with a sweet answer.

The only problem now would be to find a way to ask about the job without Jed seeing her.

Seth Yoder stood on the corner downtown waiting for the light to change; he'd just gotten off the bus from Ohio and had planned to go straight out to see Sadie, but his heart nearly stopped when he saw her rounding the corner in Jedediah Bontrager's courting buggy. He ducked behind one of the trees that lined the road and pulled his hat down to shade his face while he watched Jed park his buggy in front of the bakery.

So that's why she stopped answering my letters a year ago! She gave up waiting for me.

His shoulders sagged as he stood there watching Jed helping Sadie out of the buggy; she smiled at him, and it sent bile up his throat.

He coughed, turning his head away from the road. He shook, and a cold sweat covered him instantly as if he was about to pass out.

How could she have done this to me?

Seth walked away; he couldn't watch the two of them another minute. He strolled down the block not knowing what he was going to do. He'd sold his family farm in Ohio after burying his sickly parents, and he'd come here ready to build a house on his family's old land he'd purchased, hoping to surprise Sadie. He couldn't go back to Ohio; there wasn't a home to go back to. He'd planned to live in the loft of the barn until he rebuilt the house.

Where their house used to stand, was now a pile of ash and rubble from the argument his father and uncle had had over them leaving the community; when push came to shove, one of the oil lanterns had tipped over and set the place ablaze. The Bishop had accused his father of setting the fire on purpose and had ordered him out of the community. The barn was the only building remaining on the fifteen acres, and he was back to rebuild the house and mend his family relationship with the Bishop and the community.

One thing was certain; he would need a buggy if he was going to get around, and the only place he could get that would be from Sadie's father. He'd likely sell him a horse too, but after seeing Sadie with Jed, Seth didn't feel up to go crawling to her father for anything. He swallowed hard the pride that seemed stuck in his throat. He'd rather purchase the buggy now while Sadie wasn't home, though the very thought of having to deal with the man who didn't approve of him made his stomach churn even more than it was now.

He had no other choice but to get a ride to Sadie's house to barter with her father and then go to his land as planned. Sadness consumed him at the thought of living in the same community with Sadie and watching her marry Jed and raising a family with him. He and Jed never got along—mostly because he was a very vain guy and he didn't treat women like human beings; he treated them like they were his property and needed to obey him. Seth was more than surprised to see Sadie with

Jed; had he been her only alternative to marry because she'd waited for him for so long? He knew why Jed was still single, but Sadie must have waited as long as she could until she had to decide to keep waiting or become a spinster.

Even if he'd wanted to come for her sooner, he couldn't have. After his father died of a heart attack, his mother lost her will to live and fell sick with the flu and never recovered. Seth knew she gave up because she didn't want to live without her husband anymore, but he would miss them both dearly. His older brothers had agreed to let him sell the farm, and they each took their share. Seth had used his portion to purchase their old farm in this community, a piece of land that was a third the size of his family farm in Ohio, but it was all he could spare since he needed the rest to rebuild the house. With no bride, he didn't even feel like building a house now. Perhaps he could resell it and stay in the barn until it sold.

By the time his cousin, Elmer, showed up at the diner where he told him he'd be waiting, Seth was more than eager to get out of town and avoid Sadie and Jed.

They rode in silence to the Beiler farm except for an occasional bit of news from Elmer about how tall his corn was or the new batch of Rhode Island Reds he had running around the chicken coop. Seth didn't feel like talking; he was too busy swallowing his pride in preparation for purchasing a buggy from Mr. Beiler.

When they pulled into the driveway, Sadie's father was outside in the corral rounding up a horse. He'd written a special letter to her father and sent it ahead letting him know he'd be arriving today and that he'd need a buggy and a horse; he assumed the horse was for him. He'd also asked him not to tell Sadie so he could surprise her—only, he was the one who'd gotten the surprise.

Elmer pulled up to the barn where Mr. Beiler had tied up the horse, and the two of them hopped out and followed him into the barn. Seth shook a little wondering how he was going to ask the man about seeing Sadie in town with Jed; surely, he'd gotten his letter since he seemed to be readying a horse.

Sadie's father looked up from over the top of his glasses and frowned. "I'm making you an invoice now for the buggy and the horse."

"But we didn't agree on the price," Seth said.

The man's scowl deepened. "I charge the same for everyone," he said handing him the invoice. "The buggy and the horse are outside the barn. If you disagree with the price, you can go to another community. You don't belong here, anyway."

Seth felt his heart speed up. "I promised Sadie I'd come back to marry her and I plan on living up to my word."

Mr. Beiler snatched the glasses from his face and tossed them on his work bench. "You're too late! She's betrothed to Jedediah Bontrager, and you are forbidden to see her."

Seth pulled several bills from his pocket and tossed them on the work bench next to the man's glasses and exited the barn to hitch his buggy. He had no intention of arguing with the man when he didn't believe him; he would go straight to Sadie and make her tell him the truth.

CHAPTER TWO

Sadie tried being nice to Jed, knowing it was the only way she was going to get out of marrying him; if he didn't suspect her, then he'd relax and perhaps she'd be able to get away with what she was about to attempt. She smiled at him as he helped her down from the buggy and thanked him when he held the door for her when they went into the bakery.

"What are you going to order?" she asked, forcing a cheerful tone. "It all smells so *gut*—just like *Mamm's* kitchen."

He nodded and pointed to the layer cake in the glass display case. "Does this mean you will be serving me the sweets *before* my meals once we are married?"

The question made her quiver with disgust, but she forced a smile. "If that's what you want."

He chuckled. "I told your *vadder* you'd warm up to me; it was only a matter of time." He nudged her. "I knew you couldn't resist my charming personality."

More like obnoxious! Sadie thought, fighting the urge to make a gag motion to him to show how wrong he was.

Instead, she smiled and humored him, keeping her mind on finding a way to speak to the manager about the job.

"Would you like to sit in the park and have our treat, or would you like to stay in here where it's nice and cool?"

24

"I wouldn't want the air conditioning to spoil you and make you think you wanted to live like an *Englisher,"* he answered. "I think we should take our things outside and enjoy the sunny afternoon."

She tried her best not to let her emotion show on her face; if they left right after ordering, it would be difficult for her to get away from him. Once they left, they'd cross the street to the park, and there would be no opportunity to inquire about the job. She'd have to think of an excuse and fast—before the line moved up because they were next.

She spotted another *Help Wanted* sign standing up on the counter beside the cashier and thought maybe if perhaps he thought it was *his* idea for her to have the job, that could work in her favor.

She pointed to the sign. "They need help," she said with her biggest smile. "If I worked over the summer, then I would have a sizeable dowry by the time we got married at the end of the season."

He didn't answer, and it made her shake; he seemed to be thinking about it. Then he nodded slowly. "Your *vadder* did give his apologies that he didn't have anything set aside for you; I think it's a *gut* idea that you want to help but I am the *mann,* and I should provide for you when we are married."

Her heartrate was all over the place. "I agree with you, but we aren't married yet, and it would be a shame if I entered into our marriage with nothing to give you."

He smirked. "Having you would be enough!"

She pursed her lips and started to reprimand him, but he was already ordering; she'd been so preoccupied she hadn't noticed the people in front of them had finished.

The cashier looked at her and smiled. "What will you have besides the job in the back?"

The cashier winked at Jed, and it started to irritate Sadie, but then it made her think she could make that work in her favor.

"Did I hear you tell her she couldn't get a job?" the cashier asked. "If she works here, she gets free treats, and when you come to visit her on her break, you get them too!"

Sadie felt her heart sink to her shoes. That wouldn't lure him; he could get all the free baked-goods at home, and even her house, for that matter.

"If she couldn't take a break when you come in, I could make sure you had everything you need."

The girl smiled at Jed again, and that did the trick. It only irritated her that she'd just realized her own father would want her to marry a man who would obviously never keep his eyes or his hands to himself. She doubted he'd be faithful even if she did marry him. She'd heard all the stories about Jed, and he'd made his way through almost all the young women in the community. Sadie had been his last stop and his last hope to get married. She'd been the only one who hadn't gotten taken in by his false charm. He was a liar, and a smooth-talker and those traits did not make him a good match for marriage to anyone.

Jed turned to Sadie and smirked. "This girl has a point—I'm sorry, what is your name?" he asked, turning to the cashier.

"I'm Erin!" she said with a smile that made Jed forget all about Sadie.

"That's a pretty name," he said with his smooth tone. "Who does she need to speak to about the job?"

It made Sadie laugh internally; if that's all it takes to get rid of Jed, maybe her working here with Erin is the key to getting rid of him—or at least distracting him away from her own plan. Either way, she didn't care because it seemed to be working in her favor.

Erin looked at Sadie. "You're Amish, right, so I'm assuming you know how to bake from scratch?"

Sadie nodded, trying not to appear insulted at the girl's assumption just because she was Amish. "*Jah,* I've been baking since I was tall enough to reach the oven."

The girl nodded dumbfoundedly but forced a smile. "I don't see a problem then; the owner has hired plenty of Amish, and they always work out. Let me finish your order since you're the last person in line, and then I'll get Jake for you—he's Mr. Barnes son, the owner of the bakery."

She ordered a chai tea latte and a cranberry-orange scone, and then Erin took the money from Jed and disappeared into the kitchen. When she returned, she had a young and handsome man with her and Sadie thought for sure that Jed would object to her working for this guy. He was all muscles and a sparkly smile in his blue eyes. For an *Englisher,* he was quite appealing.

"This is Jake," Erin said. "He's the boss's son."

"I'm Sadie," she said. "I'd like to talk to you or your *vadder* about the job."

"Can you bake?" he asked, almost in a desperate tone.

She nodded. *"Jah,* I can bake anything you have on the menu and probably things you don't have."

He smiled, and she could see the relief in his expression. "My father left me in charge for the summer so he could go and open another bakery, and we lost both our bakers yesterday; one went on maternity leave, and the other ran off to Vegas and got married! If we don't hire someone immediately, we'll have to shut down by tomorrow when all our inventory is sold out."

Out of the corner of her eye, she could see Jed flirting with Erin, and she used that to her advantage.

"How soon can you start?" Jake asked. "On a trial basis—of course."

"Tomorrow, I suppose," she said excitedly. "What time will you need me to be here?"

"We don't open until nine o'clock when all the other shops downtown open, but the baker needs to be here around seven in the morning; is that too early?"

She giggled. "*Nee,* I have my own buggy and can be here in the morning."

Jed cleared his throat. "I'm sure you don't want to leave your horse here all day, and I doubt your *vadder* will want you driving that early alone," he said trying to sound as if he had authority over her. "I'll drive you and pick you up. How long will her shift last?"

Jake turned to Jed as if the two of them were deciding for Sadie and it irritated her, but she tried to keep the smile pasted on her face.

"The other bakers usually baked for the first four hours of the day and then they spent an hour cleaning up, so about five hours a day."

She was almost too giddy to care that she had to spend the rest of the afternoon with Jed; she would be away from him by the time wedding season approached, and that was all that mattered at the moment. Having the job at the bakery would give him less time with her, and it would give her the independence she needed—from him and her father.

"It's settled then," Jake said extending his hand to Jed. "We can fill out your paperwork tomorrow, but I'm guessing we'll have to pay you *under the table* the way we do with most Amish who've worked here in the past."

She nodded, and the two men shook hands to seal the deal; Sadie sighed with relief trying to contain her giddiness. Erin brought their order in a bag and to-go cups, and they were out the door.

From the moment they left town, Sadie had to listen to Jed going on and on about how much her paychecks would mean to their future together.

It's important for my future to get away from you! She thought.

"Did you see the way that girl at the bakery was flirting with me?" he said, puffing out his chest. "She wants to take me away from you."

Sadie rolled her eyes and looked away. *She can have you!*

"*Ach,* you're not jealous, are you?" he asked, nudging her.

"*Nee,* I trust you to be faithful to me."

That answer seemed to stump him because he finally kept quiet. Sadie looked out at the rolling landscape and enjoyed the birds and nature all around her. She was too happy about her new job to let anything Jed had to say bother her. He was trying to bait her, and she was not about to give him the chance to ruin this for her.

By the time they reached her farm, she had a whole other set of worries to contend with. She'd gotten Jed's approval, but she still had to get her father's.

"What if *Dat* won't let me take the job at the bakery?"

Was that really her voice asking Jed for help?

He patted her leg, and she flinched away without meaning to.

"Don't worry; I remember you want to keep everything between us pure until our wedding night."

She smiled nervously. "*Danki* for understanding—I—um just want it to be special."

He nodded. "And don't worry about your *dat;* I'll talk to him for you about the job. He's a *mann* so he'll understand the importance of starting a marriage with a little bit of money for things we'll need for our first winter. Since he hasn't put away anything for you, he'll have to accept that you'll have to raise that money for us. *Mei vadder* is giving us the land so he can't expect me to go out and earn the extra money we'll need. I have a *haus* to build."

Sadie didn't like the way he was speaking; Seth had always treated her like an equal and said they would work together for their future. Jed was making it sound as if she was going to work even after he married her.

She sighed; what did it matter? It wasn't like she was actually going to marry him!

She bit her bottom lip to cover her thoughts; he was going to handle her father, and for that, she was grateful. He was doing her a favor without even realizing it.

CHAPTER THREE

Sadie was almost beside herself with excitement over her new job. Jed had managed to convince her father that she needed the job to start their marriage off the right way and he'd actually agreed with him.

"You don't fool me, Sadie," her mother said.

She bit her bottom lip to keep the gasp from escaping her lips.

"I know you're up to something," her mother continued as she drained the bacon. "You don't want that job in town to help Jed; I know you don't care for him and I'm sorry about that, but none of us can help that Seth didn't come back for you."

Sadie bit back tears while she stirred the scrambled eggs that were nearly finished. She didn't want to talk about this now; her father would be inside with the morning milking any minute, and if he caught them in the middle of such a conversation, he'd never permit his daughter to leave their farm until the day she married Jed.

"I'm sorry he didn't come back, but Seth is a *gut mann;* I'm sure he has a *gut* reason."

She turned around and looked at her mother; she'd never heard her speak in favor of Seth before. Behind the woman's concerned eyes was a smile.

"Are you getting the job because you plan to go after Seth?"

Sadie felt her heart pound faster and her shoulders tightened. She hadn't thought of going to look for him.

"*Nee,* what if he's married someone else after all this time?"

"Seth never struck me as the sort of *mann* to break a promise," she said quietly.

Sadie turned off the flame beneath the eggs and gave them another stir.

"What are you saying, *Mamm?*" she asked, turning around to face her mother.

"I'm saying that you should follow your heart—but if you tell your *vadder* I said that, I'll deny it."

Sadie threw her arms around her mother and giggled happily. "*Danki, Mamm.*"

"I want you to be happy," she said sadly. "I was forced into an arranged marriage with your *vadder,* and I wasn't in love with him the way a bride should."

Sadie's eyes grew wide, and she covered a gasp with a hand over her mouth. "I didn't know that."

"I grew to love your *vadder* very much, but I cried a lot our first year of marriage; I too was in love with someone *mei vadder* didn't approve of. That's why I want you to follow your heart; you deserve to be happy, and I know that won't be with a *mann* like Jed."

"I'm so glad you understand," Sadie said.

"Understand about what?" her father's gruff voice startled her.

Sadie turned to face her father, unable to find her voice.

"About her new job," her mother spoke up.

Her father wagged his finger at her. "I expect you to turn over every one of your paychecks to Jed!"

Sadie's breath hitched. She couldn't do that or else she wouldn't have the money to get away from him. Then she remembered Jake said he'd have to pay her under the table. It would take her longer to save, but maybe she could find a way to keep some of the cash hidden from Jed and her father.

Anger filled her at his comment; how could he so unfair to her?

"Sadie can be trusted to hang onto the money until he's her husband," her mother said gently.

Danki Mamm for sticking up for me!

She didn't dare say the words out loud, but her mother could see in her eyes how much she appreciated it.

"I suppose you're right," her father agreed. "It might keep him from backing out of the marriage. You'll turn it over to me, and I'll keep it for you until you're married and then I'll give it to Jed for safe-keeping."

That was it; her blood was boiling. "I'm not a *boppli;* I can keep my own money*,* " she cried before running out of the room. She ran up the stairs and put on a clean apron and then ran outside to walk toward town; she didn't even intend to wait for a ride from Jed or her breakfast. She'd probably be grounded when she returned home, but at least she'd have one full day of freedom beforehand.

Her stomach growled, but then she remembered Erin telling her that she could eat free on the days she worked there; it was a good thing because she wasn't about to go back home just to eat.

Before she'd gone very far, she heard a buggy from behind her, the gelding's gate wide, his strides long. She didn't need to turn around to know it was Jed coming up from behind her; she would guess that her father sent him after her. It was obvious that she wouldn't be allowed to make any decisions for herself as long as she resided under her father's roof. Her mother had told her to follow her heart, and that was exactly what she intended to do. She had a plan for her life and Jed was not a part of that plan. Sadly, neither was Seth.

When Jed approached, she turned around, trying her best to be nice; he had, after all, smoothed things over with her father so she could get the job.

"Your *vadder* sent me to get you and take you home," he said.

Her mouth dropped open. "I'm not going home; I'm going to my new job," she said, realizing she could sway Jed to her side of the argument. "It's for my dowry— remember?"

He didn't have to know that her dowry would not be to marry him; she prayed it was to marry Seth, but she needed Jed's help. He'd threatened to take her on their date yesterday by force if necessary. The last thing she needed was to have him putting her in the buggy and taking her home to be disciplined like a child.

"Get in; I'll take you to the job, and I'll come back and talk to your *vadder* when I return."

"Danki," she said, climbing in the buggy next to him.

He clicked his tongue to his gelding and set off toward town, and Sadie was quiet the entire way there. She tuned out Jed's chatter about their future plans; she wasn't any more interested in hearing about that than he would be to hear what she was thinking. The truth was, she couldn't get her mind off Seth. She was excited to be starting a new job, but for her mother to finally tell her what she thought of Seth, well, she couldn't get it out of her mind.

She could never love another man; Seth was the one her heart cried out for.

When they reached downtown, Jed pulled up in front of the bakery and stopped his horse. "Do you want me to go in with you?"

Sadie had to bite her bottom lip to keep from squealing the word *no* at him; instead, she shook her head and smiled. "I'll be fine; you and *Dat* worry too much."

She went to hop down from the buggy when her eye caught a man across the street going into the diner. Her breath hitched; he looked like Seth, but she couldn't be sure since she hadn't seen him for almost five years.

"What's wrong?" Jed asked, looking over at the diner.

She laughed nervously. "Nothing; I'm just a little nervous. It's my first day, but I better go in alone."

Jed furrowed his brow at her and told her he'd be back for her at noon. She went inside, and Jake waved her toward the back so they could get started baking.

Seth noticed Jed dropping Sadie off at the bakery and was tempted to go across the street, but he thought better of it and let his growling stomach rule him at the moment. Besides, if she was with Jed, did he really want to see her? Of course, he did; he still loved her, but his heart was breaking, and he was still in denial about the entire thing. As long as he avoided her, he wouldn't have to hear it from her own lips that she'd stopped waiting for him and had chosen to court Jed.

Then another thought occurred to him; what if she was merely getting a ride from him and she worked at the bakery? He found it difficult to believe her father would let her out of his sight that long, but a lot of years had passed. Surely, if she and Jed had already married, she wouldn't be working there, and there was no evidence Jed had begun to grow out his beard.

He let out a loud sigh as he took a seat in one of the booths; he was letting his imagination run wild with ideas before he even knew what the situation was. The waitress brought him a menu and a glass of water, and he looked up to greet her—and Jed, who'd just walked up to his booth.

"Seth Yoder; looks like you came back from the dead!" Jed said with a mean chuckle. "Maybe it would have been better off if you'd stayed there."

Seth felt his blood boiling, but he pasted on a smile and beckoned the man to join him.

Jed scowled at him, and the waitress excused herself.

"I hope you don't think you can come back here and take Sadie away from me," Jed warned him.

Seth clenched his jaw and rose from his seat; he hadn't realized Jed was shorter than he was until he stood. It wasn't by more than about half a foot, but it seemed enough to intimidate Jed.

"Take her away from you?" Seth asked, standing as tall as possible.

Jed took a step back and looked him in the eye. "We're betrothed."

Seth felt his stomach twist in knots at the word *betrothed,* but he kept his expression as calm as possible. They weren't married yet, and he needed to hear it from Sadie's mouth—not Jed's. Not with him standing here with his chest all puffed out trying to challenge Seth; he'd bide his time until he could get the truth from Sadie, herself.

He and Jed had never been friends, and it didn't seem that the years had grown the man up any; he was still the same crass bully, but if he was still a womanizer the way he had been in their teen years, Seth feared for Sadie.

"Don't get your feathers in a ruffle," Seth said. "I'm only here to build *mei haus* on our old property; I bought it back from the bank."

"Why stay here? It ain't like you're wanted in this community."

Seth could feel his patience wearing thin; he was in no mood to debate with Jed as to his position in the community. If need-be, he intended to atone for the way his father had left things with people here. There were a lot of words said the day they left, and Seth had been just a little bit too young to stay here on his own. As much as he'd wanted to stay for Sadie, he couldn't provide for her then—but now he could—unless she was truly spoken for. Nonetheless, he'd promised his father on his deathbed that he'd come back and make amends on his behalf and buy back the land that he'd fought his brother Abe over. He'd never forgiven Abe for making him sell their family land, nor the Bishop for suggesting they sell it to end their feud over ownership once their parents passed away. Seth was here to fix all of that and make up for the sins of his father if need-be.

"I have my reasons, and I don't owe you an explanation. I intend to stay, so keep your empty threats," Seth warned him.

"They're not empty," Jed shot back. "You keep clear of Sadie, or I'll have you thrown out like your worthless *vadder!*"

Seth flinched, but he didn't throw a punch the way his instincts begged him to. He was here to fix things—not make them worse. Fighting with Jed would only add to the bad blood between his family and this community.

"You leave me alone, and I'll leave you alone," Seth said. "How about that?'

Jed nodded. "That suits me just fine, but that goes for Sadie too; she's going to be my *fraa* soon, and I don't want the likes of you trying to soil her reputation by trying to see her."

"I'll keep my distance," Seth agreed.

He didn't mean it if he could help it, but he didn't intend on making trouble with Jed. He'd barely been back for twenty-four hours, and already trouble was finding him in more ways than one. Doing his father's bidding was going to require him having an iron stomach, and he wasn't sure he was up for the task.

"See that you do," Jed gave his final warning before exiting the diner.

Seth didn't understand what Sadie could possibly see in Jed, but he was willing to bet her father was behind their engagement.

CHAPTER FOUR

Sadie tried her best to shake off the feeling of uneasiness she felt about thinking she saw Seth; she knew if he were in the community, her house would have been the first place he would have stopped. She was anxious about her new job, and her mind was playing tricks on her—that's all there was to it. At least that's what she hoped was wrong.

She paid attention while Erin showed her how to work the mixer and the oven, and showed her where everything was. For her, all she needed was a counter, bowls, and utensils and she could make anything they needed her to from scratch—with or without the mixer, and she preferred to do without it. To her, the machines would only slow her down. She could make anything as fancy or as primitive as they needed it to look. Jake had shown her the samples to give her an idea of what each product should look like to make it presentable in their display case. He left her to her job, and she was prepared to get into the baking zone and do what she did when she had a lot on her mind. Baking was her passion—the one thing in her life she could count on to keep her mind occupied. Her *mammi* used to tell her that if she ever had a problem, it could all be worked out in the time it took to knead a batch of bread.

She'd made plenty of bread since Seth had left the community and the only thing it had managed to do was to take her mind off it for a while. Right now, she needed to do just that; her priority was to earn enough money to do what her mother had suggested, and that was to go to Seth and see for herself why he didn't come back for her. Whatever the reason, she was prepared to face it—even if it broke her heart more than it already was.

Jake walked out of the office to check on her. "Whatever you have in the first set of ovens is making my mouth water," he said.

Her stomach growled, reminding her she'd left the house without her breakfast. "*Danki,*" she said quietly. "I'm almost ready to put the loaves of banana bread in there now."

"After that, maybe you can make some of those pies you were telling me about."

"The *snitz* pies?"

He nodded and rubbed his belly with a smile. "We can make that today's special. I'm going to go up front and have Erin put it on the menu board."

Sadie went back into her zone; she could bake with her eyes closed. The bakery was abuzz with employees, and each of them seemed to know exactly what tasks needed to be done, and Sadie liked how well everyone worked together. They were all so friendly and had helped her with any questions she had.

Her first shift seemed to fly by, and before she realized, Jed was there to pick her up. She'd had such a wonderful day, and now that he'd shown up, her stomach was full of knots again. She wasn't looking forward to being in his company on the ride home; more than that, she had no idea what mood she'd find her father in when she returned. There would be a punishment for the way she'd stormed off that morning, and she prayed it wouldn't mean the end of her job here.

"What's wrong?" Erin asked her as she was cleaning up her work space.

"I had so much fun here today; I don't want to leave."

Erin laughed. "It is a nice place to work; the Barnes family is good to their employees. You don't look very happy with your boyfriend though; did the two of you have a fight?"

The girl looked almost hopeful, and it made Sadie chuckle internally, but she wouldn't wish Jed on an enemy, much less a friend.

"I'm not sure *mei vadder* is going to let me keep this job," she blurted out, unable to keep in her angst a second longer.

"You're old enough to decide that for yourself!" Erin commented.

"Not as long as I live under his roof."

Erin shrugged. "So move out."

"I don't have anywhere else to go," Sadie complained. "So I have to do what he says."

"I'll bet Jake would let you have the other loft apartment above the bakery," Erin said with a smile. "I'm staying in one of them; we'd be living across the hall from each other."

Sadie shook her head. "I don't have the money for that."

"You don't have to," she said. "Mr. Barnes takes out a portion of my salary every week to pay for the apartment, and it's fully furnished."

Sadie thought about it for a minute; it might take her a little longer to save the money she needed, but that would be better than having her father and Jed controlling her. It would probably break her mother's heart if she left, but she was the one who encouraged her to follow her heart.

She looked up at Jed, who was waiting impatiently by the counter.

Erin looked at him too. "Don't worry; I won't tell your boyfriend."

Sadie sighed. "He's not my boyfriend; *mei vadder* is making me marry him."

Erin frowned. "You don't like him? He seems charming enough."

"He's certainly charming," Sadie said with a lowered voice. "But don't let that fool you; he's not very kind."

Erin smiled. "A bad-boy, huh? I could tame him!"

Sadie had to keep from laughing. "No woman in our community has been a match for him, but maybe an *Englisher* could make a difference."

"He's so good looking!" Erin said with a smile.

Sadie looked at him again. "He's physically handsome, but his personality doesn't match."

"That doesn't bother me much," Erin admitted. "I'm a little shallow."

They both giggled.

Jake came over to them and smiled. "Congratulations, Sadie, your *snitz* pies are a hit with the customers."

"Danki."

"Hey, Jake," Erin said. "Can Sadie take the other loft apartment upstairs? She might need it."

Sadie felt her heart pounding wildly; she wasn't going to ask about it, but Erin was a pretty outspoken person.

Jake nodded. "We could work out the same deal Erin has with us if you need it.'

"Danki," Sadie answered. "I'll let you know tomorrow or the next day if that's alright.'

Jake nodded. "Works for me. Thank you for making so much today; our inventory was getting low."

She nodded and smiled and then took the last of her mixing bowls and utensils back to the sink to the dishwasher.

"What were you chatting on about so much back there when you knew I was waiting for you?" Jed barked at her once they were on the road toward home.

Sadie felt her heart skip a beat; had he heard what they'd been talking about?

"Nothing, really," she said as casually as possible. "The manager was thanking me for all the things I baked today and told me how much the customers liked my *snitz* pies."

"I didn't like the way he was looking at you," Jed said. "Are you sure he wasn't trying to flirt with you? Because that's the way it looked from where I was standing."

Sadie bit her bottom lip to hide her anger. "He wasn't flirting with me; he is the boss, and he needs to talk to the employees, and he wanted to see if I needed any special ingredients to make specialty items like the *snitz* pies."

"Are you sure he isn't taking advantage of your baking skills because you're Amish?"

Sadie guffawed. "*Nee!* Why would you say such a thing? They're paying me a salary just like the other employees. I wasn't treated any differently today."

"I'm going to keep an eye on him; he needs to know that money is for our wedding."

Sadie gulped. He was not going to let that go; was he?

The closer they got to her farm, the more her stomach tightened. "Did *mei vadder* say if he was going to let me keep the job?"

Jed glared at her. "He shouldn't after the way you acted this morning, but I was able to convince him you were nervous about your first day and that we will need that money for the winter."

"*Danki,*" she said quietly.

Sadie bit her bottom lip; it was bad enough she had to suffer the reprimand from her own father, but to get it from Jed made her blood boil.

When they pulled into the driveway near the barn, her father poked his head out and then disappeared back inside.

"Go in the *haus,*" Jed ordered her. "I want to talk to your *vadder.*"

Sadie was getting tired of being ordered around and talked about like she was a child, but she kept her mouth shut and did as he told her to without bothering to tell him goodbye.

She stormed in the house and collapsed angrily into the chair, her mother at the sink with a welcoming smile.

"Tell me what's wrong," she said.

"There aren't enough hours left in the day to tell you what's wrong," Sadie huffed. "I'm so upset; I think I saw Seth in town today!"

Seth finished clearing away all the debris out of the basement of his old house, which was all that remained after the fire. It seemed to be in good shape, and he could salvage it for the foundation of the new house. He would begin framing the walls tomorrow, but he would have to hire help by the end of the week once it came time to raise the framing. He planned to bring in pre-fab trusses for the roof, which were cheaper and easier than building them himself. He hoped to have the exterior finished before autumn rains hit; he could move in as soon as he had the roof put on and the windows secured.

He lifted his head thinking he heard an approaching buggy. Propping the ladder back against the cement wall, he climbed out of the basement and looked out toward the road. A young female pulled into the yard and parked near the barn. She stayed in the seat until he walked over to her.

"I'm Jesse Bontrager," she said. "Do you remember me? *Mei mudder* asked me to extend a welcome meal to you since you're our new neighbor."

He looked into her familiar face. "Are you Jedediah's *schweschder?"*

"Jah," she said with a smile.

Seth was leery of taking food from her, thinking Jed might have sent her.

She extended her hand to him, and he assisted her out of the buggy. She pointed to the large basket of food in the back and asked him to get it out for her.

She grabbed a quilt from under the seat of what looked like Jed's courting buggy. "We can sit under the tree over there in the grass and eat if you'd like."

We? Does she want to eat the meal with me? I guess if she's going to eat it too, then there isn't anything wrong with it!

"Ach, that's fine," he said clumsily.

What could he say to her? Thanks for bringing me food, now please go home! No, that wouldn't go over too well. It was kind of her to bring it and even kinder of her mother if she really had suggested it. It made him wonder though if her mother knew who he was; he hadn't exactly had the welcome mat put out for him by the community. Maybe if he was lucky, the people had forgotten what his father and uncle had done, or perhaps didn't hold him accountable for their actions. Either way, his growling stomach was grateful for the meal.

"*Danki* for the food," he said. "I picked up a few snacks in town today, but it isn't exactly a meal."

She spread the blanket beneath the tree and sat down. Seth put down the basket and sat at the far edge of the quilt. He wondered if her mother had given her permission to join him; she looked young, and he tried to remember how old she might be now. They'd been neighbors growing up, but since he and Jed had not been friends, he couldn't be sure how old the girl was. For that reason alone, he didn't intend to give her a reason to infer anything about them sharing a meal.

She unpacked fried chicken, a container of mashed potatoes and gravy, a jar of chow-

chow, and a large Mason jar of lemonade. Seth peeked inside the basket when she lifted out the plates and saw another container that looked as if it had a few slices of pie in it.

"You'll have to thank your *mudder* for me," he said, taking the plate she'd dished out for him. He set it in front of him on the quilt and waited until she had her plate fixed. Then he bowed his head for a silent prayer.

When he finished, she poured glasses of the lemonade for them. "I'm turning eighteen in two days, and I'd like to invite you to my party," she said enthusiastically.

He nearly choked on his lemonade. He took in a deep breath and forced a smile. "I'm not sure if I'll be able to; I've got so much to do before the rainy season starts back up."

"I'm only inviting *familye* and my close friends," she said. "But I understand if you can't make it; it is short notice."

At least now he knew how old she was; only two days away from marrying age!

Lord, please let her be here for the reason she said and not because Jed is trying to distract me away from pursuing Sadie by using his schweschder as bait.

Seth kept his mouth as full as possible so he wouldn't have to do much more than nod at her constant chatter.

"I can bring you supper every night if you want me to," she offered.

Seth was thankful he didn't have a mouthful of food at that moment, or he'd have likely spit in out in front of him. Instead, he took another bite of the fried chicken hoping to divert her attention away from an answer. The chicken was good, and the offer very tempting, but he supposed the invitation came with her as a dinner companion, and he did not want to give her the wrong impression about the two of them having a future together.

"*Mei mudder* already said it was alright if I did that—to be neighborly—since you don't have any place to live yet,"

He gulped down the mashed potatoes in his mouth. "I've been staying in the barn, and it's cozy in the loft, but you're right about needing to find an alternative way to eat. I thought about making a fire pit or even purchasing a barbeque grill in town to cook on, but I still wouldn't have a place to store meat so it won't spoil."

"How about until you figure it out, I can bring you supper in the evenings," she offered.

Seth thought about it. "Only if you let me pay you for your trouble," he said.

She frowned as if he'd insulted her. "Pay me?"

"I'd have to pay for a meal if I went into town," he argued. "If I paid you, it would be kind of like a *job* for you."

"I'm not sure *mei mudder* would like that idea."

"At least let me pay for the food," he offered. "I have to go into town tomorrow for lumber, and I can give you some money to buy the food, and you can plan a menu for the week for me; how does that sound?"

She perked right up and smiled. "*Jah,* I'm sure *mei mudder* would be alright with that."

He smiled, wondering which of them was getting the better end of that deal—him because he would be getting regular meals, or her because she'd be taking a *buggy ride* with him into town. She didn't seem like the devious type, but she was related to Jed, and he could charm the birds out of the trees.

Lord, I hope that wasn't the wrong decision.

CHAPTER FIVE

Sadie sat across the table from her father waiting for him to say the prayer over the food; she'd gone without two meals today, and she was salivating over her mother's baked chicken.

Her father raised his head and picked up the knife and fork to carve the chicken. "You know, the more you resist Jed, the tougher your marriage will be."

There isn't going to be a marriage between us, she thought.

She kept her head down and began to gobble the food on her plate. By the time she'd gotten home today, her mother had already had most of the meal prepared, which would leave her to do the dishes this evening. She suspected she'd be doing dishes most evenings from now on with her new job. He'd not mentioned her leaving the job, so she suspected Jed had warded him off the subject of her quitting for the time-being, which also meant she wouldn't have to leave home and move into the loft above the bakery. She almost hoped he'd object to her holding down the job so she could leave. It was time; she was old enough to be on her own, but she knew that once she left, there would be no coming back if she needed to.

A knock at the door startled her; usually, no one would show up this time of the day. Her father rose from his chair and went to the door.

"Sorry I'm a little late," she heard Jed say. "But I had to drop off a few things at the new house."

Sadie put her fork down and gulped down the bite of food in her mouth. Her stomach soured when her father invited Jed inside to join them. He sat next to her and patted her hand under the table, but she flinched away.

"Hurry and eat," he said enthusiastically. "I have a surprise for you."

Sadie wiped her mouth with her napkin and put it over her still-full plate.

Jed looked up at her father. "Do you mind if we eat later so I can show her?" he asked excitedly. "I can't wait to show her."

Her father shooed them with his hand. "*Jah,* go! But be back before your *mudder* puts all the food away."

Sadie didn't move; she flashed her mother a helpless look, but the woman lowered her gaze.

Danki, Mamm, for sticking up for me when I really needed you to. Her sarcastic thoughts didn't do anything except fuel her anger as she rose from her chair reluctantly.

Where was Jed taking her, and why wouldn't her mother speak up on her behalf?

Jed helped her into his buggy, and she sat there feeling defeated; were both her parents against her happiness? It seemed as if her mother wanted her to be happy this morning, but it was evident to her now that her father had influenced her back to his side since she'd been at the bakery all day.

They rode in silence past a few familiar farms until they passed the old Yoder place. Sadie turned her head when she spotted two buggies in the yard. She squinted her eyes against the setting sun searching for who belonged to the buggies until her gaze fell to the large oak tree in the yard.

"Seth!"

She hadn't meant to say it, but there he was sitting under the tree having a picnic with—with Jesse, Jed's younger sister. Her mouth hung open, and her eyes widened, her mind unable to process what she was seeing with her own eyes.

"I thought you knew he was back!" Jed said with a chuckle as he slapped at the reins of his horse to make him pass the farm at a fast trot.

"He came back to marry Jesse," Jed said.

Sadie craned her neck to get another look at the intimate picnic and felt her heart lurch forward and seemingly bounce onto the road in front of Seth's old house.

"What?" she squealed without meaning to. "Since when is Seth marrying Jesse?"

"He's been writing to her for about a year now," Jed said with a chuckle. "I thought you knew that."

Sadie turned her head away from the cozy couple, who hadn't even noticed them driving by. Her own letters from Seth had stopped coming about a year ago; it was obvious now why he'd stopped writing to her. Was *this* the surprise Jed had for her?

"That's your past," Jed remarked with a grin. "Your future is up ahead a little further."

She pasted on a bitter smile and turned her head, swallowing hard against the tears that heaved inside her.

Landscaping blurred past her but time seemed to stand still; her mind flooded with the promise Seth had made to her five years ago, and the promise she'd made to wait for him. She'd waited, and he hadn't; had he been biding his time for the past year waiting for Jesse to turn eighteen so he could marry her? She knew they were neighbors all that time, but she never thought the two of them knew each other—especially since he was five years older than she is. She was just a girl when Seth left the community; no matter how much Sadie tried to make sense of what she just saw, she couldn't imagine when or how he'd become betrothed to Jesse.

She sat there biting the inside of her cheeks, not wanting to cry in front of Jed; it would only anger him, and then he'd likely tell her father, and then she'd be reprimanded by him too, and she wasn't in the mood for any of it.

Jed pulled the buggy into a long driveway of a house she knew to be for sale, but the sign was no longer in the yard. Her heart hit her ribcage with a thud; he'd mentioned being at the *new* house when her father had let him in the kitchen door while they were eating supper.

"What do you think?"

Jed's excitement caused her to jump.

Sadie stared without seeing, unable to think past the vision of Seth and Jesse sitting under the oak tree having a picnic.

"What do you think of the *haus?*" Jed repeated himself.

"For what?" she mumbled, trying to keep her lower lip from quivering.

"I bought the *haus*—for us to live in when we get married," he said, hopping down from the buggy. "It needs a little work, but I think I can have it livable before the wedding—with your help, of course."

Sadie unblurred her eyes and really looked at the house. The windows were broken, and the porch roof was sagging; the yard was overgrown and the paint faded. It was going to need a lot of work, but not by her hands.

Jed reached a hand up to her, and she climbed down from the buggy and stared at her future; she was going to marry Jed and live in this house and be miserable for the rest of her life. She was never going to laugh at Seth's silly jokes anymore, and she wouldn't see his smile every day for the rest of her life. She was doomed to spend her life in tears, and the permanent frown on her face would match the world she'd live in.

He led her up to the house, and she followed robotically.

"Hey, what's with the blank stare?" Jed asked. "I'm showing you the house we're going to live in, and you don't seem very happy."

"I don't have anything to say," she mumbled.

"Well, you could start with saying *danki* for buying you a *haus!*" Jed barked.

Sadie's breath hitched, and her emotions poured out all at once. "I'm happy for you that you have a new *haus,* but I'm sorry; I don't want to marry you," she sobbed. "I've already told you I don't want to marry you, but you and *mei vadder* don't listen. I have to listen to my heart, and it's telling me not to marry you."

She ran off toward the road not caring what Jed or her father thought; it was obvious now that she'd completely rejected Jed that she would have to pack her things and leave her father's house.

When she passed Seth's old house, he and Jesse were no longer sitting under the tree; there was only one buggy remaining on the property—a buggy her father made. Her heart sped up as she examined more closely the horse hitched to the tree—it was in the corral up until a few days ago. She recognized it by the white mask on his face.

She stopped for a minute and bent forward to catch her breath; it made her shake to think that Seth had been at her house to buy a buggy and a horse, but no one had told her he'd been there—not even her mother. She shook her head, her fingernails digging into the palms of her tightly-closed hands. They'd lied to her—all of them—including Seth.

It was dark by the time she reached her father's house, and she stood outside willing herself to go inside, but she couldn't. Jed hadn't bothered to go after her; she supposed his pride kept him from doing so. She hadn't wanted to see him and needed the long walk home, but now as she stood here, she didn't want to see her family either.

The kitchen door swung open, and her father stepped out into the night air. "Where is Jed? I didn't hear the buggy pull into the driveway."

Sadie's breath heaved with anger. "He isn't here, *Dat;* I left him at the house after telling him I won't marry him."

"You *will* marry him; it's a smart match," her father barked.

"Why didn't you tell me Seth was here to buy that horse with the white mask—and a buggy?" she demanded.

His face twisted into a scowl. "Don't you raise your voice with me. I don't have to answer to you about my business; I can sell to anyone I please. I told him to leave the community and stay away from you; he's not right for you."

Sadie blew out an angry breath. "His money is *gut* enough for you, but he's not *gut* enough for me? Isn't that what you mean?"

"Go in the *haus,*" he hollered, pointing his finger toward the kitchen door. "You go to your room and don't come out until you can apologize to me for the way you spoke to me and until you agree to marry Jed."

"I have to work tomorrow at the bakery, and you can't make me marry Jed; I don't love him. Don't you care?"

"You will learn to love him, and if you refuse to marry Jed, there is no reason for you to have a job."

Sadie ran into the house and past her mother, who called after her, but she didn't stop until she reached her room upstairs at the end of the hall.

She threw herself on the bed and sobbed for several minutes before a knock at her door forced her to sit up and decide if she had the strength to answer it. She knew it was her mother; her father would have pounded on the door just before bursting into the room. She rose from the bed to let her mother in; she wanted to hear what the woman had to say about the matter.

When she opened her door, her mother pulled her into her arms and allowed Sadie to sob on her shoulder.

She smoothed her daughter's hair and shushed her. "I'm sorry I didn't tell you Seth was here; I'm caught in the middle of the feud between you and your *vadder* and he's a hard *mann* to live with. It is right for me to stand in agreement with him, but deep in my heart, I can't agree with hurting our *dochder* this way. I know you love Seth and you deserve every happiness this world has in store for you. Go to him and talk to him."

"I can't, *Mamm;* I saw him having a picnic with Jesse—Jed's little *schweschder.* Jed says he's been writing to her for a year now, and that was the same time my letters stopped coming from him—do you remember? Jed says Seth came back to marry Jesse."

"Do you really believe that?" she asked.

Sadie broke away from her mother and collapsed onto her bed and hung her head. "I have to wonder," she sobbed. "I saw them together tonight when Jed drove me to that *haus* he bought; did you know about that?"

Her mother nodded. "I heard the two of them talking about it over *kaffi* this morning after he dropped you off at the bakery."

"*Dat* said I have to quit my job there," Sadie cried. "I don't want to quit."

Her mother sat beside her on the bed and pulled Sadie's hand into hers. "You shouldn't have to, but I don't know how you can get away with it; your *vadder* has forbidden you to go."

"There is a way," she said lifting her gaze to search her mother's reaction.

"I will help you if I can, but I don't see how you can get around your *vadder.*"

"One of the girls who works there lives above the bakery," Sadie said slowly. "There are two loft apartments up there, and the owner's son said I could rent the other one; they take the rent out of your salary."

Her mother nodded slowly as if the reality had sunk in. "I think it would be *gut* for you to get out on your own. Even if things don't work out for you and Seth then at least you won't have to obey your *vadder* and marry a *mann* you don't love."

Sadie couldn't believe what her mother was saying; she'd never heard the woman go against her father.

"Your *brudders* were so much easier," she said. "I think your *vadder* feels like he needs to be sure you're marrying a *mann* he approves of and he knows will provide for you."

"Jed is *not* a *gut mann*," Sadie cried. "Can't he see that? He's possessive and controlling and thinks like *Dat*—that I need to *obey* him."

Her mother nodded. "They do share a lot of the same traits so I can understand how difficult it must be for you to get close to Jed; you've never been close with your *dat.*"

"I don't want to have to move away from you, *Mamm,*" Sadie said. "But I don't plan to quit my job—even if I have to defy *Dat*—I'm an adult, and I need him to treat me like one."

"How are you going to get into town?"

"I'm going to take my buggy and my horse," she answered. "If *Dat* objects to me taking my own horse then I will walk the five miles."

"That is a long way; maybe I can help by distracting him in the morning for you. I'll make his favorite breakfast, and he will be too busy eating to notice you're not sitting with us."

"What if Jed shows up?"

"Maybe it would be best if you left a little early," her mother suggested.

Sadie nodded and hugged her mother; it felt good to have someone on her side, but she worried her mother would suffer a lecture followed by a long period of the *silent-treatment* from her father. For some reason, Sadie didn't think her mother cared too much about that; she seemed more concerned about her daughter.

CHAPTER SIX

Seth drove Jesse into town with him; he dropped her off at the grocery store and promised to pick her up when he finished his errand. After seeing Sadie and Jed ride by his house last night when he was having supper, Jesse had confirmed that the two of them were betrothed. Today, he decided, he was going to find out the truth for himself. If he heard it from her own lips, then he would respect that, and he'd not try to pursue her, but if it was all a big misunderstanding and they weren't betrothed, he wanted to know.

He pulled his buggy up in front of the bakery and parked. Then he tied his horse to the parking meter and dropped a quarter in it and twisted the dial. He stared at the time it gave him in disbelief.

"Ten minutes?" he grumbled, jiggling his pocket for another quarter—just in case.

With twenty minutes in the parking spot, Seth walked into the bakery, the bell on the door chiming when he entered. The scent of sugar and cinnamon hit him as he stepped into the lobby, but Sadie's homemade banana nut bread made his mouth water. He would recognize that warm aroma anywhere; her breakfast bread would lure him to her house every morning when they were growing up, and he'd trade her fresh goat's milk for a loaf. On the days she made goat cheese from the milk, he'd sit on the back porch with her and enjoy a slice of bread with the cheese spread on it. She was a very talented baker, and he hoped the owner's of the bakery appreciated the bargain they were likely getting for the salary they were paying her. To Seth, her baked-goods were priceless.

He moseyed up to the front counter and spotted Sadie in the back, twisting dough into pretzels. He raised a hand to wave when her gaze lifted and met his. She frowned and then went back to what she was doing, ignoring him.

Erin nudged her and pointed to Seth. "I'm guessing he's here to see you," the girl said. "He's even cuter than the other one; what's your secret? I can't get even one guy to chase after me!"

Sadie bit her bottom lip to keep from smiling; Seth had seen her do it a million times before. It was what she did when she didn't want to give up her mood and smile.

"You're due for a break," Erin said. "I've watched you twist hundreds of these; I think I have it by now and I can finish the batch."

Sadie pursed her lips and hesitated. "If you're sure—I'll only be a minute."

"Good luck!" Erin said with a giggle.

Sadie held up a finger to Seth and motioned for him to meet her outside, and then she disappeared out the back door of the bakery. Seth walked out and went toward the end of the building and turned down the alley where she was pacing back and forth and mumbling to herself. It tortured him to see her so stressed out, and he assumed it was because of him.

She turned around to face him when he approached, her face twisted in anger. "Just how long were you going to wait before telling me about you and Jesse getting married?" she barked at him. "Are you only here because I saw the two of you having a cozy picnic at your old *haus?*"

"*Ach,* you saw that?" he asked, removing his hat and raking his fingers through his dark blonde hair. "What about you? Carrying on with Jed of all people. Jesse told me the two of you were betrothed."

Sadie hung her head.

"Then it's true?" he asked, his pitch a little higher.

She shrugged and forced a smile. "Not exactly."

"How can you *not exactly* be engaged to someone?"

He could tell she was searching for the right answer, but she was coming up short, and he was losing his patience.

She stopped pacing and leaned her back against the brick building. "*Mei vadder* is making me marry him because he didn't want me to marry you. He said you'd made me wait too long without any word from you and…"

"I wrote to you every week!" he interrupted.

"*Jah,* for the first four years," she said. "But then I found out that you've been writing to Jesse for the last year and…"

"I never wrote to her!" he interrupted Sadie again.

She sucked her breath in, and her eyes grew wide. "Well, you didn't write to *me* all that time either."

"What are you talking about?" Seth asked. "I wrote to you every week; when is the last time you got a letter from me?"

"About a year ago—about the same time you started writing to Jesse."

His jaw clenched. "For the last time; I've never written to Jesse; I hadn't seen her or talked to her once over the past five years— until last night when she brought me supper— at her mother's insistence."

"Why were you having a picnic with her?"

"She invited herself to eat with me, and I couldn't be rude after she brought me a meal; I would have refused the meal except that I don't have any way to cook yet at my place and I was really hungry after a hard day of getting the foundation ready to build on."

"So you aren't going to marry her?"

Seth guffawed. *"Nee!* I wouldn't even date her; she's too young, and I don't love her."

"You don't?" she asked with the smile he'd missed so much.

"Do you love Jed?"

She flashed him a disgusted look and shook her head. *"Nee,* I don't."

His heart leapt from his ribcage, seemingly reaching out for Sadie's. He'd never stopped loving her. She'd grown more beautiful than he'd remembered if that was possible; her blonde hair was already sun-kissed, and her blue eyes stood out against the slight pink in her cheeks.

"Your *vadder* told me you and Jed were betrothed and said I was forbidden to see you."

"It's not true," she said.

"I'm glad to hear that," he said with a smile.

He closed the space between them, pressing his hands against the brick wall behind her head. He was so close to her he could feel her breathing, his face so close, the temptation to taste her lips was almost too much for him.

Sadie felt a fluttering in her stomach when Seth closed the space between them; he had her trapped between himself and the brick wall, but she had no desire to flee. Her lips parted, but she couldn't speak; her breath was heaving with excitement.

"Tell me you still love me," he whispered, his smoky baritone sending shivers all the way to her toes.

Her lashes fluttered. "I do love you," she said with a quiet moan.

Seth leaned into her and pressed his lips to hers, the warmth of them sending a spark of heat that ignited the fire in her belly. His mouth swept across hers and then moved toward her cheek, where he placed a gentle kiss. His lips found her earlobe, his warm breath tickling her with desire for more.

"I love you, Sadie," he whispered. "I came back here to marry *you.*"

Her breath hitched, but his lips swept down her neck, rendering her unable to concentrate on anything else. She tipped her head back slightly, and he nuzzled her collarbone with his lips.

"Marry me, Sadie," he begged her in between kisses.

"Yes!" she moaned, moving her mouth toward his and deepening his kiss.

Her heart raced as he embraced her, pulling her indecently close. He stroked her back as he kissed her passionately. Her whole body prickled from his touch, her lips on fire, her breathing profound.

"Sadie!" a female voice squealed.

It broke the spell between them, and they broke apart, each standing at attention. Sadie's heart pumped so hard she coughed to catch her breath. Unable to get her bearings right away, she hadn't realized that Erin was calling her from the back door of the bakery.

"You better get in here," she said. "That other Amish guy is standing at the counter waiting for you, and he looks angry!"

Sadie flashed Seth a pleading expression.

"Go!" he suggested. "We have a lot to talk about later."

Before she could protest, he leaned in for another quick kiss on her cheek and hurried down the alley.

Sadie bit the inside of her cheek to keep from smiling as she followed Erin into the bakery—especially after the girl nudged her playfully and waggled her eyebrows at her. They'd shared a brief giggle before going inside, and it was difficult for her to contain her giddiness over Seth's impromptu proposal.

Then it hit her; he'd delivered on his promise after all, just like she'd prayed for. What confused her was why Seth took off so hastily and left her to deal with Jed on her own.

She supposed when they talked later, she'd understand more then, but for now, she was happy about her proposal, and her lips still tingled from Seth's kiss.

After straightening out her hair behind her prayer *kapp,* she went up front to meet Jed. Her giddiness turned quickly to angst when she looked into his angry eyes; she suspected he was about to make a scene, and she was grateful Jake had stepped out of the bakery to run some errands in town and would not be there to witness whatever was about to be discussed between them.

"What were you doing outside?" Jed barked. He didn't even wait for her to approach him.

Her heart sped up at his question, and she could feel her cheeks heating; he would surely tell her father—not that it mattered because Jake had told her when she arrived for her shift this morning that the loft apartment was hers if she needed it.

"I was getting some fresh air," she said. "I needed a break from breathing in all that flour."

It wasn't a lie, but it wasn't the whole truth either.

"My next question is; what are you doing here after your *vadder* has forbidden you to work here?" he demanded. "Don't you know this could hurt our chances to marry?"

Sadie jutted out her chin and narrowed her eyes. "I don't owe you or *mei vadder* an explanation, and for the last time; I'm *not* marrying you."

Jed clenched his jaw and leered at her. "You *will* marry me!" he growled.

"You can't make me marry you," Sadie said, standing her ground.

Jed smirked at her and left the bakery.

"What was that all about?" Erin asked, coming up behind Sadie.

Sadie shook her head in disbelief. "He still thinks I'm going to marry him after I've told him and *mei vadder* that I don't want to."

"The way he stormed out of here; do you think he's up to something?"

Sadie bit her bottom lip and shrugged. "I hope not."

Jesse came bursting into the bakery and caused Sadie to jump and turn around.

"Have you seen my betrothed?" she asked impatiently.

"I didn't know you were engaged," Sadie said, trying to keep a straight face.

She furrowed her brow. "You know I'm engaged to be married to Seth Yoder. I'm finished getting his groceries and was looking for him to take me back home."

Sadie's eyebrows raised. "His groceries?"

Jesse rolled her eyes and clucked her tongue. "*Jah,* so I can make shoofly pie for him to go with our supper tonight."

Sadie felt her heart pounding with the force of stampeding horses; shoofly pie was his favorite and Jesse was making it for him. Had he requested it?

"You're making him supper again tonight?" Sadie asked, trying her best to keep her tone even.

"That's what you do when you're betrothed," she said. "You obviously don't understand that since you have refused to cook for *mei brudder.*"

"Probably because he is not my betrothed," Sadie retorted.

"I'll expect the two of you at my birthday party tomorrow night," Jesse said, ignoring her comment. "I'll be announcing my engagement to Seth."

Sadie gulped. "Seth is going to be there—at your party?"

"Of course, silly! He's my betrothed; why wouldn't he be there for my special day and our special announcement?"

Sadie felt her heart twisting in a knot. Had Seth just tricked her into admitting she loved him and had no intention of following through with his promise to her?

"*Jah,* I'll be there," Sadie said methodically.

She wasn't about to miss the big announcements; it would either give her relief that this was all a nightmare, or closure once she learned the truth.

CHAPTER SEVEN

Sadie went home after a long day at work; Jake told her the toilet was leaking in the loft apartment and he wouldn't be able to get a plumber there to fix it until the following day, and he'd had to turn off the water. Though she was disappointed, she understood but feared what would be waiting for her when she got back home and had to face her father. She didn't expect her mother to stand up for her; she had to live with him after Sadie left if that was what it would come to. She felt sorry for her mother in some ways, but she was so set in her ways, Sadie couldn't do anything to help her.

Her heart sped up the closer she came to her parents' house, and she was tempted to drive by Seth's to see if they could talk but it was already late, and if she wanted to stay at home for another day or so, she would need to go home and try to cooperate with her parents. Helping her mother with the evening meal would go a long way toward mending the broken fences between her and her father.

She pulled into the yard and hopped down to unhitch her horse when her father's voice startled her.

"You disobeyed me, Sadie and I want an explanation!"

Her heart felt as if it was trying to leap from her ribcage, and her limbs shook, but she had to act like a grownup and stand her ground without trying to be disrespectful to her father.

"I didn't wait for Jed this morning to give me a ride into town," she answered. "I wanted to take my own buggy because I had errands to run and didn't want to make him wait."

He pondered her answer. "That was considerate of you."

"I'd like to drive myself from now on, so I don't take him away from his work on the new *haus*," she added, hoping he would think she was still considering marrying Jed.

He nodded. "It does need a lot of work before you get married. He can't expect to bring home his new bride to a *haus* that's unlivable."

Sadie nodded in jest; did he *really* still believe she was going to go along with this marriage to Jed? She wanted so much to share her news about Seth, but she didn't trust her father not to yell at her some more or to forbid her to see him.

"Let me finish with the horse," he said. "You go inside and help your *mudder;* she spent most of the afternoon making a batch of cookies, so she's probably a little behind with supper."

"Cookies?" Sadie asked. It was unusual for her mother to bake; she'd usually had her do all that.

"*Jah,* she made them for you to take with you to Jesse Bontrager's birthday party tomorrow night."

Sadie felt a tightness in her chest. "I wasn't planning on going to her party; I don't really care for the girl, and I don't know her."

"It's about time you got to know her," he barked. "She's going to be your in-law soon."

She is not! Sadie thought.

"I'll be too tired to go after working all day and coming home to help *Mamm* in the kitchen."

He narrowed his eyes. "You will go to that party, or you will quit that job if it's too much for you to extend a kindness to your soon-to-be *schweschder.*"

Sadie stood there trying to decide if she was going to argue with her father or let it go; she would be able to stay in the loft apartment starting tomorrow night, so she didn't have to come home *or* go to the party. Then she remembered about Jesse and the big *announcement* she was making and changed her mind.

"Do I need to hitch up the horse and take you downtown to quit that job?" her father asked firmly.

She shook her head. *"Nee,* I'll go."

He turned back to the horse and finished unstrapping him, ignoring his daughter since she'd given into his demands.

Lord, forgive me for arguing with mei vadder. Please help me to find a way out of all the messes I seem to keep getting myself into.

"I'm sorry, Sadie, but the plumbing isn't fixed; it was worse than I thought," Jake apologized. "I'm afraid it won't be fixed until tomorrow. It wasn't only the toilet that was leaking, but the pipe beneath the floor too. It's a good thing we caught it though before it caused the bakery to shut down."

Sadie felt her heart sink to her shoes; now she would have to go to Jesse's party tonight with Jed. There would be no talking her way out of it with her father. It wasn't what she'd wanted to hear at the end of her shift; she'd hoped she could go upstairs and relax in her new apartment. Instead, she would have to go back home and succumb to her father's demands for another day.

"You're welcome to move your things into the apartment anytime you'd like," Jake offered. "But the water won't be back on until the pipes are fixed."

"Danki." She had brought most of her clothing with her today thinking she would not be going back home, and it would be better if she left it here.

Erin took her upstairs with the key after she got her small bag of things out of her buggy.

"You don't have very much," Erin commented.

"I was glad to hear that the apartment was furnished because what I have in my bag is all I have that belongs to me."

Erin flashed her a look of disbelief that quickly turned to pity.

Sadie shrugged it off; she knew *Englishers* had more material possessions than the Amish did, and it didn't matter to her. She would be content in the quaint little apartment.

"The furniture is a little old-fashioned," Erin said. "But it's free with the place, and the kitchen has small appliances, but there are pots and dishes." She pointed out everything in the place and showed her the small bedroom and bathroom.

Excitement rose from Sadie's gut; she was excited about the place and wished she could stay tonight.

"After work tomorrow you'll be an independent woman," Erin said with a giggle.

"I wish it were tonight, so I didn't have to go to that party with Jed," Sadie complained.

"Do you want me to go with you?" Erin offered.

Sadie giggled. "*Nee,* I need to be brave and face my fears. *Danki* for the offer though."

"Alright I get it," Erin said. "But I could keep Jed busy for you so you can enjoy the party."

"I don't think I'm going to enjoy it no matter what; I'd rather be able to spend the evening with Seth. I haven't been able to talk to him about yesterday. I'm a little confused about his friendship with Jesse."

"I'm sure there's a good explanation for it," Erin said. "I could see genuine love in his eyes for you. A man like that wouldn't betray you."

"I trust him—and not just because I know what a liar Jesse can be," Sadie said. "But that doesn't mean I'm not worried she's trying to sink her hooks in him."

"Do you worry she'll succeed?"

Sadie shook her head and smirked. "*Nee,* not a chance!"

Erin turned the key to lock the apartment door behind them. "Then stop worrying."

"You're right; I'm making more of this than it is; I'm sure of it."

Erin smiled. "Let's get this key back to Jake so you can go back to your parents' house."

Her comment struck Sadie a little funny, but she supposed she was right. That was her parents' home and no longer hers; she'd grown up and was about to be independent.

Seth readied himself quickly so he wouldn't be late for Jesse's birthday party. After the girl had let it slip that Sadie would be there with Jed, he aimed to find out why. He'd been tied up all day with his house, and he'd hoped he'd have time to get away and see her at the bakery today, but he'd gotten his first lumber delivery today, and he'd been eager to get the first section of wall framed before dark. He'd have a lot of work to do before he could get a roof on the house, and he prayed he could do the work by himself and still get done before the autumn rains hit. Not to mention the fact that Sadie had accepted his proposal and for that reason alone, he was eager to get the house built. The sooner he finished, the sooner she could become his bride.

He went out of the back of the barn where he'd rigged up a temporary shower by re-routing the plumbing. He still had to use the outhouse, but that would only be temporary. Seth patted his horse before hitching him to the buggy. He'd put on his Sunday best; Sadie had always favored a royal blue shirt and black broadfall pants on him. He'd put on his best black hat and shined his shoes for the occasion, and he felt confident he would get to the bottom of Sadie's connection with Jed. He wished he had someone to divert Jed's attention away from Sadie, but he was willing to take his chances that he could talk to her without Jed making a scene in front of the members of the community.

Though he and Jed had had words, he'd let it go when he realized Jesse's interest in him. Seth wasn't stupid; he knew that Jed hoped Jesse would keep him busy and keep him from pursuing Sadie. He wouldn't put it past Jed to be the one behind Jesse's sudden obsession with cooking for him.

Once his horse was hitched to the buggy, Seth hopped in and set off toward the Bontrager home. They lived close enough that he could have walked there, but he didn't want to get his shoes dirty or be all sweaty once he arrived from walking. He hoped to steal a kiss or two from Sadie and talk to her more about his letters and why she thought he hadn't sent them. He suspected her father intercepted them, but he didn't want to accuse the man without proof. To do so would only hurt Sadie, and he would never do anything to hurt her purposely.

He turned into his neighbor's driveway and pulled in a deep breath. He felt a little nervous about what to expect inside the house with all the guests. He had no idea Jesse was that popular, but there must have been twenty or more buggies parked in the yard already, and the night was still early.

He tethered his horse to the hitching post that ran the length of the two large oak trees in their yard. Since they had the biggest barn in the community, church was usually held at their farm. Had been that way since he could remember. For that reason, they had put in long hitching posts for the community members to park their buggies in the oversized front yard of their home.

He pulled in another deep breath and walked toward the front door of the home where several people were gathered.

A couple of them greeted him kindly but seemingly began to whisper once he was clear of them. He tried not to let it bother him; he wasn't here to prove anything to anyone. His main goal tonight was to see Sadie and get the answers he needed.

He went inside and was immediately assaulted with a series of squeals from Jesse; he could feel the heat rising in his cheeks as she made a spectacle of herself and him. Then his gaze locked onto Sadie, who was standing near Jed and he felt anger rumble in his gut. The man was standing close enough to touch her and Seth didn't like the idea of that. Had the man ever tried to put his hands on Sadie? He prayed not, but he was certain she could take care of herself if he tried.

"I'm so glad you finally got here!" Jesse gushed.

He forced a smile, wondering exactly what to do with his shaky hands, so he looped them in his suspenders, realizing that he was the only one who was dressed up in their Sunday best. He hadn't thought that it would be a casual gathering, or he'd have put on a brown pair of pants and worn his straw hat like everyone else seemed to. He felt conspicuous in his dress clothes, and the attention Jesse was giving him didn't help.

"You're the best birthday gift a girl could ever ask for!" she swooned, trying to loop her arm in his.

He backed away from her and Jed came toward him. If there was one thing Jed knew about him, it was that he wouldn't fight with him in front of people. He could get away with saying whatever he wanted to about him, and he knew Seth wouldn't do a thing about it. When they were kids, and Jed would try to goad him into a fight, he'd accept the challenge, but Jed always became somehow mouthier whenever there was a crowd.

"Everyone," Jed said, hushing the crowded room. "Tonight is a special occasion for two reasons. First; it's Jesse's eighteenth birthday, which means she is now of marrying age, which brings me to her other big news. I'd like to welcome her betrothed to our *familye;* Seth Yoder!"

Everyone clapped, but Seth could feel the blood draining from his face, and when his gaze met with Sadie's, her face was flush, and her hand flew up to her mouth in surprise.

He couldn't find his voice with everyone hooping and hollering and cheering for him and Jesse. "Stop!" he managed to squeak out. "You've got this all wrong; I'm sorry, Jesse, but I never promised to marry you. I have to go; I don't belong here."

He bolted from the room and ran out the front door; he needed air, but more than that, he needed to get away from this place before he and Jed had a real fight.

CHAPTER EIGHT

Sadie ran out of the party, Jed fast on her heels. He grabbed her arm and swung her around to face him,

"Where do you think you're going?" he yelled in her face.

"I'm going after Seth," she squealed. "Let me go; I'm marrying him, and there's nothing you can do to stop me!"

"Maybe I can't, but your *vadder* and the Bishop can!'"

"No, you can't!" Sadie broke free from his grasp and ran toward the road, where Seth was pulling his buggy out onto the main road.

"Wait!" she hollered after him.

He stopped his horse and held out his arm to her; he slapped the reins against the gelding as soon as she was seated because Jed was running after them. The horse took off at a gallop, bouncing the buggy until they crossed over from the dirt road to the main road that led into town.

"I have to go back for my horse and buggy," she said, looking back toward the Bontrager's house.

"I have a feeling Jed will be taking it back for you," Seth said.

She turned around and leaned into his shoulder as he tucked his arm around her. "He said the Bishop and *mei dat* were going to make me marry him!" she sobbed.

"Why were you there with him?"

"Because *mei dat* made me go with him; he was going to make me quit my job at the bakery if I didn't go," she cried. "What were *you* doing there?"

"I only went because Jesse told me you were going to be there and she said there was going to be a big announcement," he said. "I thought I was going to have to break up an engagement party for you and Jed, but it turned out the two of them ambushed *me!*"

"Ach, why would Jesse think you wanted to marry her?" Sadie asked. "She was at the bakery yesterday looking for you; she told me she was making you shoofly pie for dessert after the dinner she was making you. Why was she making you dinner?"

"Because I paid her to," he answered. "I can see now that was a big mistake. She offered to make me supper and bring it over every night since I don't have *mei haus* finished and I've been sleeping in the barn. I told her the only way I would let her do that was if I paid for the food *and* her services as a cook, but she had other plans for the two of us. She wanted to get romantically involved with me, and I told her I was already betrothed to *you!* That's when she said I needed to be at her party tonight because I didn't want to miss the big announcement about you and Jed. I had no idea she and Jed were planning to turn the tables on me tonight."

Sadie pulled in a loud breath. "I can't believe how nervy those two are. They are certainly cut from the same cloth, those two."

"You've got that right," Seth said. "The problem is; what do we plan to do about it?"

"I don't see that there's anything we *can* do about it," she answered, sniffling. "They have us over a pickle barrel, and now I can't go home tonight, and my apartment won't be ready until tomorrow after work."

"Your apartment!" Seth said with a slightly raised voice. "What apartment?"

"The one above the bakery," she said. "I didn't get a chance to tell you about it yesterday because you ran off."

He nodded. "Sorry about that; I didn't want Jesse to catch me with you because I had a bad feeling about that party tonight and my hunch was right. I didn't let on about anything until she forced her hand with me."

"I'm going to be staying in the apartment loft above the bakery until we get married if that's alright."

"*Jah,* but what will you do tonight?"

"I can't go back there to get my horse because Jed will either be waiting for me, or he'll take the horse back to *mei dat* and tell him that I ran off with you. Either way, I can't go back now."

"I can't take you back with me," Seth said. "Even if I wasn't sleeping in the barn; I wouldn't want to put us at risk of going to far before we are married, so we can't spend the night together in the barn, and I don't want to give the appearance that we've sinned when we haven't. People will talk."

"*Ach,* I'll bet Erin, the girl I work with, will let me stay with her for one night," Sadie said. "We've become *gut* friends."

"That is a *gut* idea." Seth pointed his horse toward town.

She was grateful it was still light out, and Seth would be able to get back home before dark if he didn't take too long telling her goodnight.

"*Danki* for taking me all that way," she said, leaning into his sturdy frame.

He pulled her close and kissed the top of her head and breathed in. "I've missed the sweet smell of the homemade honeysuckle soap you use on your hair. I've missed everything about you, and it would take a lifetime of holding you before I'd ever take it for granted."

She giggled and nuzzled under the comfort of his arm.

By the time they reached the bakery, Sadie had nearly fallen asleep on Seth's shoulder; she was so comfortable and content with him, and she had fallen in love with him all over again yesterday when he'd kissed her. She'd never stopped loving him, but so much time had passed since they'd ignited the sparks between them, she'd worried over the years if they would get that newness back. For her; that newness was back with an extra dose of love because he'd finally made good on his promise.

Seth parked the buggy and helped her out; he walked her down the alley and toward the back steps that led to both loft apartments.

"I don't know if I like the thought of you living here all alone and being alone at night," he said, looking up toward the landing where both doors to the loft were.

"Don't worry," Sadie assured him. "The whole building has a security system, and both loft apartments have their own code and a key to get in."

"That makes me feel better."

She leaned in and kissed him lightly on the cheek. "Besides, Erin will be right across the hall from me if I need anything."

"Go on up and see if she's home and if she'll let you stay," he suggested.

Sadie left him at the bottom of the stairs while she went up and knocked on the door.

"Sadie; what's wrong?" Erin asked when the door swung open. "You look like you've been crying!"

"I have," she sniffled. "It's a long story, but I can't go home, and you already know my apartment isn't ready yet; can I stay with you tonight."

Erin looked down at Seth, who lifted a hand to wave and she waved back. "You mean, you don't want to stay with that gorgeous man you just got engaged to?"

Sadie giggled shyly. "*Nee;* we're not married yet."

"Oh," Erin said, her eyes widening. "I forgot you're saving yourself for marriage."

Sadie leaned in and whispered. "You're not?"

Erin clucked her tongue and rolled her eyes. "Not on purpose! I want to really be in love first, and I haven't found what you have with Seth."

"You will," Sadie said softly. "And when you do, I'm sure you'll want your wedding night to be special."

"I never thought I'd say this, but I hope you're right about all that—saving yourself stuff."

Sadie smiled. "I am; trust me."

"You can stay here tonight if you don't mind the couch," Erin said. "I slept on it one night when my little sister stayed over, and I woke up with a stiff neck, but you're a lot shorter than I am so you should be a perfect fit."

Sadie leaned in and hugged Erin. "*Danki;* I'm going to go down and tell Seth I can stay so he can go home."

Erin winked at her. "Take your time saying goodbye; I'll be up for a while."

Sadie's smile widened, and she thanked Erin once more before going down the stairs into the alley.

Once she reached the bottom of the stairs, she threw herself into Seth's arms. He pulled her close where she felt safe and loved.

"I'm curious about something," Seth said, still holding her close. "Why did you stop writing to me?"

She pulled away and looked at him wide-eyed. "Me stop writing to you? Your letters to me stopped coming about a year ago."

Seth shook his head. "*Nee;* something isn't right. I already told you that I wrote to you every week even though I never got one letter back. When I got here, I saw you in town with Jed, and when I went to your farm to get my horse and buggy, your *vadder* told me you and Jed were engaged to be married. You looked so happy when I saw you."

"Don't pay attention to that; I was only trying to be nice so that *mei dat* would let me work at the bakery. Before we left *mei haus* that day, we'd had a terrible fight. That was the first time I told him I wasn't marrying him; he doesn't listen unless it's something he wants to hear. I think he and *mei dat* would make a perfect *vadder* and son." She giggled. "At least then he would be *mei brudder,* and he wouldn't be chasing me around the hen *haus. "*

"Ach, didn't you tell your *dat* that you didn't want to marry him?"

Sadie nodded. "I told him about a hundred times, but he gave me another lecture about how Jed and I are a smart match, and that I need to get my head out of the clouds, and face the fact that you were never coming back to marry me—and he went on and on about how bad you are—and how bad your whole *familye* is. He was not kind, but those are his words, not mine; I'm sorry for his words about you."

Seth shrugged. "It only bothers me that he was trying to turn you against me; I know what a *gut mann mei vadder* was, and his memory doesn't deserve to be tarnished with such harsh words against him."

Sadie's breath hitched. "His memory?"

Seth nodded. "He and *mei mudder* both died."

Sadie frowned and a lump formed in her throat. "I'm so sorry for your loss."

"*Danki,* that means a lot to me, and it would have meant the world to *mei mudder.* She knew I'd be coming here to find you once she passed and so she asked me to tell you that she would always love you. I had both *mei* parents' blessing to marry you."

Tears dripped down Sadie's cheeks; she pushed out her lower lip and tilted her head to the side. "Aww; that means so much to me. *Danki* for telling me."

He reached up and wiped away her tears with his thumbs. "This is not a sad occasion; it's a happy one, so let's put away the tears and give me a kiss goodnight before you retire with your new roommate. Do you need me to bring you anything tomorrow when I come to see you after work?"

She shook her head. "*Nee;* I already put my clothes and personal things in the loft apartment, so I won't need anything. But I would like some company if you'd like to visit and see the place."

"I'd like that," he said with a smile.

"What about your dinner companion?" Sadie asked.

"If you invite me to dinner tomorrow, I'll have a new one—the one I'd prefer."

She giggled. "You better!"

He laughed and pulled her close, his resonance becoming more sincere. "I love you, Sadie, and I can't wait to marry you."

"Me too!"

"Why do we have to?" Seth asked. "Your *vadder* will surely shun you if you marry me—if you're prepared for that—I'd like to take you downtown and marry you tomorrow if you'll have me."

"You mean to get married without friends and *familye?*"

"Jah," he said. "All they do is complicate things and put expectations on us."

"I will," she squealed. "But I'd like to get word to *mei mudder* to give her a chance to witness us getting married."

Seth nodded. "I'd love for her to be there, but don't be surprised if she says no."

"I know she could, but I'm not going to worry about that; I'm too excited to worry about anything beyond what I'll wear. I don't have a blue dress."

"Then wear violet," he suggested. "I have a violet dress shirt so I can match you."

Sadie smiled. "Can I wear daisies in my hair?"

He nodded. "They would be beautiful, but they would pale in comparison to your beauty."

Sadie felt herself blush and she was glad it was getting dark enough that he probably couldn't see well enough to notice.

"*Danki,*" she said shyly.

Seth moved in and began to kiss her goodnight, but she had a feeling it was going to be a long night in the alley with him, and there would be more than one *goodbye* between them.

CHAPTER NINE

Sadie stretched and yawned, leaning her head from side-to-side. Her neck was stiff from sleeping on the sofa in Erin's apartment, and she was exhausted from crying sad and happy tears both, but today was her wedding day.

She smiled.

Nothing was going to upset her today—not even her father or Jed. Seth would be in town to pick her up at one o'clock after her shift at the bakery ended and they would go to the courthouse to get married.

She heard Erin's alarm clock going off in the other room, and her friend groaned as she turned it off. She'd promised to give her a ride in her car over to her parents' house so she could tell her mother about the wedding and invite her.

Moments later, she had coffee brewing, and Erin poked her head out of her bedroom door. "Are you all done in the bathroom?"

Sadie nodded. "*Kaffi* should be ready any minute."

"Good!" Erin commented with a sleepy tone. "I need to wake up before we go."

Sadie waited until the coffee maker finished and then poured two cups and added a little creamer from Erin's fridge. She smiled again as she stared out the window into the horizon where the sun was just beginning to gleam between the buildings. The park across the street was still lit up with the lights that illuminated the fountain, but soon, the sun would make the water sparkle even more than the multi-colored lights.

Within a few minutes, they were on their way to Sadie's family home. She twisted her hands in her lap as she watched the landscaping whizzing by in a blur. They would be there in only a few minutes by car, and she wasn't sure if she was prepared to face her father if she should encounter him.

"Let me off at the base of the driveway," Sadie pointed out to Erin. "I don't want the car to alert *mei vadder.*"

Erin pulled over on the shoulder of the road behind a thick patch of pine trees and turned off the engine, and then wished Sadie *good luck.*

She pulled in a deep breath and walked up the driveway toward the side to keep herself hidden behind the tree line. If she could slip inside the kitchen door without her father seeing her, she'd breathe a little easier, but the kitchen door was too risky. It was too close to the barn where her father would likely be this time of the day. Instead, she cut through the trees in the front yard and made a beeline for the front door. Pulling the key from her apron pocket, she slowly turned the lock and opened the door. She remembered too late that it creaked at the midway point; her father's voice came rambling from the kitchen.

She was caught.

"Why are you sneaking in the *haus* like a…"

The Bishop, who was at his side, put a hand on his arm to stop the word, but she knew what he was about to call her; she could see it in his face.

Jed came in from the kitchen, and her heart felt as if it dropped into her shoes.

"We have listened to Jedediah's confession," the Bishop said gently. "We need to listen to yours and then we can proceed."

Sadie's eyes darted between her mother, who had sad tears in her eyes, and her father, who was wearing his usual scowl, and then to Jed, who was wearing his usual smirk of satisfaction, and back to the Bishop, who had reprimand in his eyes.

"What is it that you think I need to confess?" she asked.

"Spending the night in Jed's arms in an unholy manner," the Bishop said.

Sadie's breath hitched, and her hand flew to her mouth, her eyes widening as her gaze locked with Jed's. Her eyes narrowed, and her jaw clenched.

"What did you tell him?" she demanded, her fiery eyes fixed on Jed.

He shrugged and pressed his lips together to hide the grin that Sadie hadn't missed. "I told him the truth, and you'll feel a lot better once you confess too, and then the Bishop said he'd wave the baptism and marry us so that we won't sin anymore."

Sadie pulled in a breath and let it out in a squealing whoosh. "How dare you tell such a lie about me! I spent the night above the bakery last night in the loft apartment with the girl I work with; her name is Erin, and she's waiting in her car at the end of the driveway for me. I would *never* spend the night with such a vile *mann* as Jedediah Bontrager—

especially when I'm engaged to be married to Seth Yoder—who is a *very* honorable *mann,* contrary to what *mei vadder* believes."

"That will be enough!" her father barked.

"I *know* you kept Seth's letters from me for the past year and made me believe that he didn't love me anymore," Sadie cried. "Do you have *any* idea how much you hurt me? I used to cry myself to sleep thinking that Seth had betrayed me and broken his promise to me, but it was *you* who broke your promise to me! When I was little, and I was afraid of the dark, you used to tuck me in at night and tell me you would always protect me from harm. What you failed to promise me was that you would not protect me from your own agenda for my life. You failed me, *vadder,* because you broke that promise to me by trying to force me to marry this liar and bully—*jah, Dat,* Jed is a bully and a liar—but he reminds me a little of you!"

Her father's eyes misted up, and Jed made an aggressive move toward Sadie; her father put his arm out to block Jed.

"You're my betrothed, Sadie, and you won't shame me by carrying on with Seth behind my back!" Jed yelled at her through gritted teeth.

"Do you have anything to confess to me?" the Bishop asked her.

Sadie shook her head. "*Nee,* I have done nothing wrong, and I can prove it; my friend is outside, and she can back up my story."

The Bishop turned around and looked at Jed who'd lowered his gaze. "You apologize for your lies and then go out to my buggy and wait for me."

"I'm sorry," he grumbled without looking up.

After Jed left the room, the Bishop turned to Sadie and pulled her hands into his. "I believe you; Jed has always been a troubled boy—ever since his *vadder* passed away, but maybe with some counseling from me, he'll straighten up. Don't hold his sins against him; I have a feeling he lied because he doesn't like losing things—but you are a person with feelings, and you didn't deserve the lies he's told about you. It seems there might be a little mending to do in this *haus* too. If you need anything, let me know."

With that, the Bishop said his goodbyes to her parents and left.

Sadie wiped a tear from her eyes and waited for her father to speak; he wouldn't even look at her.

After a few minutes of silence, she couldn't take it anymore and went to her mother and hugged her. "I'm getting married today at the courthouse to Seth Yoder because I love him and I'm going to follow my heart just like you told me to."

"What about the baptism?" her father barked without looking at her.

"If we decide to join the church, we will take the classes together and get baptized," Sadie answered him. "If not, I guess you'll have to shun me."

Her mother pulled her into another hug. "I love you," she whispered.

"I love you too, *Mamm;* I love you both. I'm getting married today at three o'clock, and I'd like you to be there—both of you."

She kissed her mother on the cheek and paused to wait for a reaction from her father; when she got none, she left the house and ran down to Erin's waiting car to take her back to town. She'd spoken her piece; the rest was up to her parents.

CHAPTER TEN

Sadie's shoulders shook as she opened the car door; she slid into the seat of the car and closed the door, covered her face with her hands and began to sob.

"Oh my gosh; what happened?" Erin asked.

"Jed lied about where I was last night, and he told the Bishop *and* my parents that I spent the night with *him!*"

Erin clucked her tongue. "That liar! What did your parents say?"

"I think *mei mudder* believed me but *mei vadder* didn't say a word to me and I don't think he believed me," she sobbed. "The Bishop made Jed apologize to me, so I think *he* believed me."

Erin patted her arm. "I'm so sorry; do you want me to go up there and tell them the truth?"

Sadie shook her head. *"Nee,* it won't do any *gut;* once Seth and I are married, we'll be excommunicated from the church, and I suspect *mei vadder* intends to shun me, which means by association, *mei mudder* would have to shun me too."

Erin gasped. "That's awful! Why would your own parents do that to you?"

"It's a form of punishment; no different from *English* parents cutting their kids off financially. It's not easy for the youth to survive without the help of their parents and the community. So they *cut you off* from them until you come back to the *familye* and the ways of the *Ordnung.*"

"Are you going to cave to that, or are you going to follow your heart and marry the man you love?" Erin asked.

Sadie sniffled and let out a little giggle. "I'm afraid today will be a bittersweet day for Seth and me, but I'm going to marry him because I know that is what *mei mudder* really wants for me. I pray that *mei vadder* will be concerned more with my happiness than with the ways of the *Ordnung,* but I suppose only time will reveal that."

"I'll pray for your family," Erin said. "I think I still remember how."

Sadie giggled. "How long has it been since you've prayed?"

"It's been a while; not since I left home."

"Well, there's no time like the present," Sadie said, grabbing hold of Erin's hand.

Sadie said a simple prayer and then let Erin say a short prayer; it was like a fresh start for both of them.

"Let's get to work before we're late," Erin said afterward.

"The day is going to drag on until Seth comes for me this afternoon."

"It's going to be a beautiful wedding," Erin assured her. "You'll see.

Seth pushed his gelding to reach the Beiler farm; he had a lot on his mind, and he didn't want to marry Sadie without giving her father a chance to give his blessing. If he said no, then at least Seth gave it a shot, but his conscience wouldn't allow him to risk her being shunned because of him.

When he pulled into the yard, Sadie's father exited the barn and scowled at him.

"You shouldn't be here," he barked at Seth.

"I came here to get your blessing."

Mr. Beiler shook his head. "I won't give it because I don't agree with it."

"I also want you to know that I forgive you for keeping my letters from Sadie," Seth said.

"I don't need your forgiveness," Mr. Beiler said, anger in his tone. "What I did, I did for *mei dochder's* sake. Your *familye* left the community, and I didn't want you to take her from me."

"But don't you see that by trying to keep her from me it only brought us closer together," Seth pleaded. "I'm going to marry Sadie today because I love her; I came back to this community to face the awful way that *mei vadder* left and to try to make up for the terrible things he said to the Bishop when he left here. He's dead now, but before he went, he asked me to make amends for him and rebuild our *familye* home here and to establish myself back in the community. I am rebuilding that *haus* because I plan to stay here. I'm not planning to take Sadie away."

"But you want to marry her before taking the baptism," he barked. "So you will be shunned."

Seth ran a hand through his thick blonde hair and blew out a discouraged breath. "I could understand shunning us if we left the community after being baptized, but we both plan to take the baptism this season, and we don't want to wait to be married until then."

"You are running off to be married in the *English* world without her *familye;* just because you don't have a *familye,* you don't think about these things."

"That is why I'm here," Seth said. "To get your blessing."

"How can I give my blessing for an *English* wedding?" Mr. Beiler asked. "You should be shunned for these actions against the church and her *familye.* "

"Then you won't see your *dochder* again," Seth said. "How can you live with that?"

Sadie's father stood there with folded arms and looked off in the distance without saying a word.

Sadie checked herself in the mirror once more and pinched at her cheeks to bring some color to her face; Seth was late!

"What if he changed his mind?" Sadie said, her voice choking up.

"He'll be here," Erin reassured her. "He might have gotten caught in traffic or something; you never know."

She sighed. "I've waited five long years for this day."

Erin chuckled. "Then waiting another couple of minutes won't make much difference."

Sadie glanced at the clock. "He should have been here long before now."

They heard footfalls on the stairs, and they looked at each other wide-eyed.

"It sounds like more than one person!" Erin said, concern in her eyes. "But don't worry; I'm sure it's him."

"You go to the door," Sadie said. "I'm too nervous."

Erin walked through the bedroom of her loft apartment and out to her kitchen where the door was. She opened the door and let Seth in, and Sadie came in the room, her breath hitching. Her groom looked so handsome in his violet dress shirt that was tucked neatly into the narrow waist of his black broadfall pants. His black hat rested over his thick blonde hair, and his blue eyes smiled along with the grin on his chiseled jaw.

Seth smiled brightly at Sadie, and he closed the space between them and hugged her. "I have a surprise for you!"

She beamed from ear-to-ear. "Your being here is enough for me; I was so worried when you were late."

Seth motioned for Erin to open the kitchen door again and Sadie burst into a half-laugh, half-cry when her parents walked in the door.

"Mamm, Dat, are you here to give us your blessing?"

Sadie held her breath while she waited for her father to speak.

He nodded. "I hope you can forgive me for intercepting your letters from Seth; at the time, I thought I was doing you a favor, but I never meant to hurt you. I was afraid of losing you, but Seth made me see that by making you choose between him and us that I almost lost you anyway, so you have my blessing for your marriage to Seth."

"*Danki*, *Dat*, that means a lot to me." Sadie closed the space between them and threw herself in her father's arms.

He enveloped her in a warm hug and kissed the top of her head. "I forgot you were not my wee one anymore. I'm sorry I broke my promise to you, but if you let me, I'll do what I can to make it up to you."

"*Ach, Dat,* I'm so happy you're here, and you give us your blessing. I love you, *Dat!*"

"I love you too," he said, his voice breaking. "I want you and Seth to live in the *dawdi haus* until he finishes rebuilding his *haus* for the two of you."

She gave her father another robust hug. "That means so much to me; *danki.*"

Sadie broke from her father's grasp to hug her mother. "*Danki, Mamm,* for telling me to follow my heart; a part of my heart will always be with you and *Dat,* but now it belongs to Seth."

"I love you, Sadie, and wish all the best for you," her mother said with a tearful voice.

"Let's go over to the courthouse," Seth said. "I'm ready to make you my bride!"

Her father chuckled—a rarity. "I can see how eager this young *mann* is to make you his bride; shall we go?"

"Wait for me!" Erin called out.

"Of course, I will," Sadie said with a giggle. "You're my maid of honor."

"Really?" Erin squealed.

Sadie nodded and smiled.

Seth took her hand and led her out to his waiting buggy while they waited for her parents and Erin to pile into their buggy. Once everyone was settled, Seth slapped the reins and pointed his buggy toward the courthouse that was three blocks down the road.

"*Danki* for getting *mei dat* to come today," Sadie said, leaning over and kissing him on the cheek.

"I couldn't marry you without your *familye* with you," Seth said.

Sadie kissed him again. "I'm grateful for that, and you've made this day even more special, but in just a few minutes, you'll be *mei familye* too."

Seth waggled his eyebrows and smiled. "I love you, Sadie, and I can't wait to make you happy for the rest of our lives."

"Being your *fraa* will be enough for me," she said. "I won't need anything else."

She sighed and leaned her head on his shoulder thinking this was the happiest she'd ever been in her whole life; she couldn't imagine being happier than right now in this moment.

Not only had her parents both shown up for her special day, but they were going to build their home in the community just the way Seth had promised her all those years ago.

THE END

Special offers…

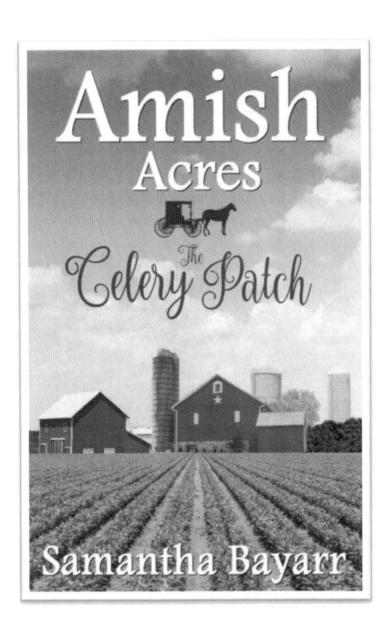

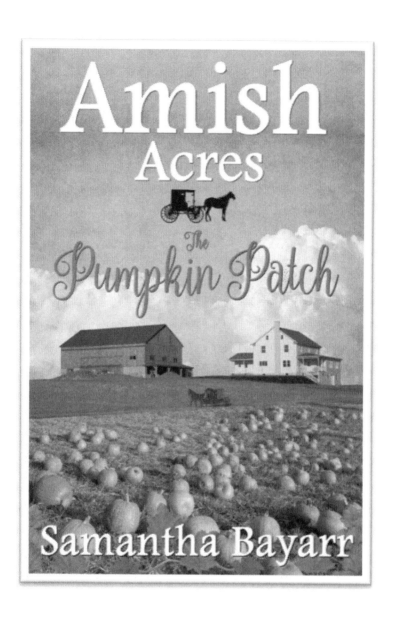

Amish
Acres
The
Pumpkin Patch

Samantha Bayarr

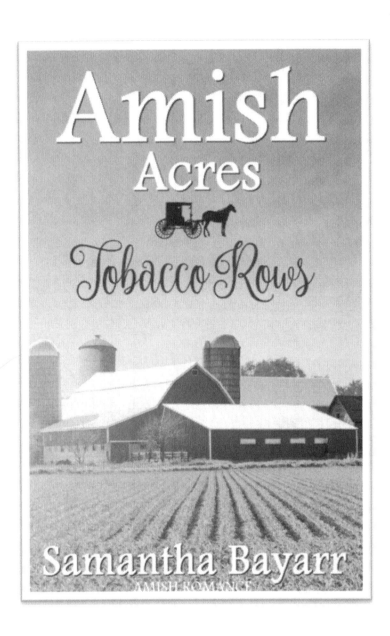

Amish
Acres

Tobacco Rows

Samantha Bayarr
AMISH ROMANCE

Amish Weddings Collection

Samantha Bayarr

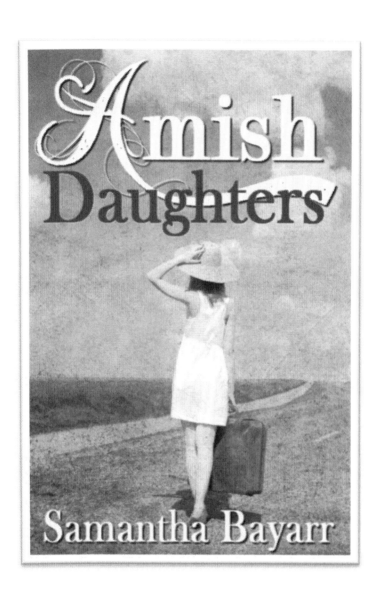